Charro de Oro

andrés indaburu

Ordering Information:

Prime Seven Media
518 Landmann St.
Tomah City, WI 54660

Printed in the United States of America

Alasito never had a thing.
Not even a real name.

Don Seferino found him on the
street when he was a baby.

He loved him
so much.

It was so sad when he got
hit by that streetcar.

Left nothing behind but debts...
And Alasito stopped smiling...

Cried a lot, caught a
cold and died as well...

Son!

It is not your time yet!

You shouldn't be here! This is shadowland!

Don't be afraid to live.

When Alasito came back from the dead,
Doña Sulpicia had already bought his
coffin, and told him he was going to
pay her one way or the other.

She was mean to him.

Fed him cold soup
and stale bread...

We don´t eat until we get
back home.

Anybody can fall. But not everybody can get up right after.

Get up! Damn you!

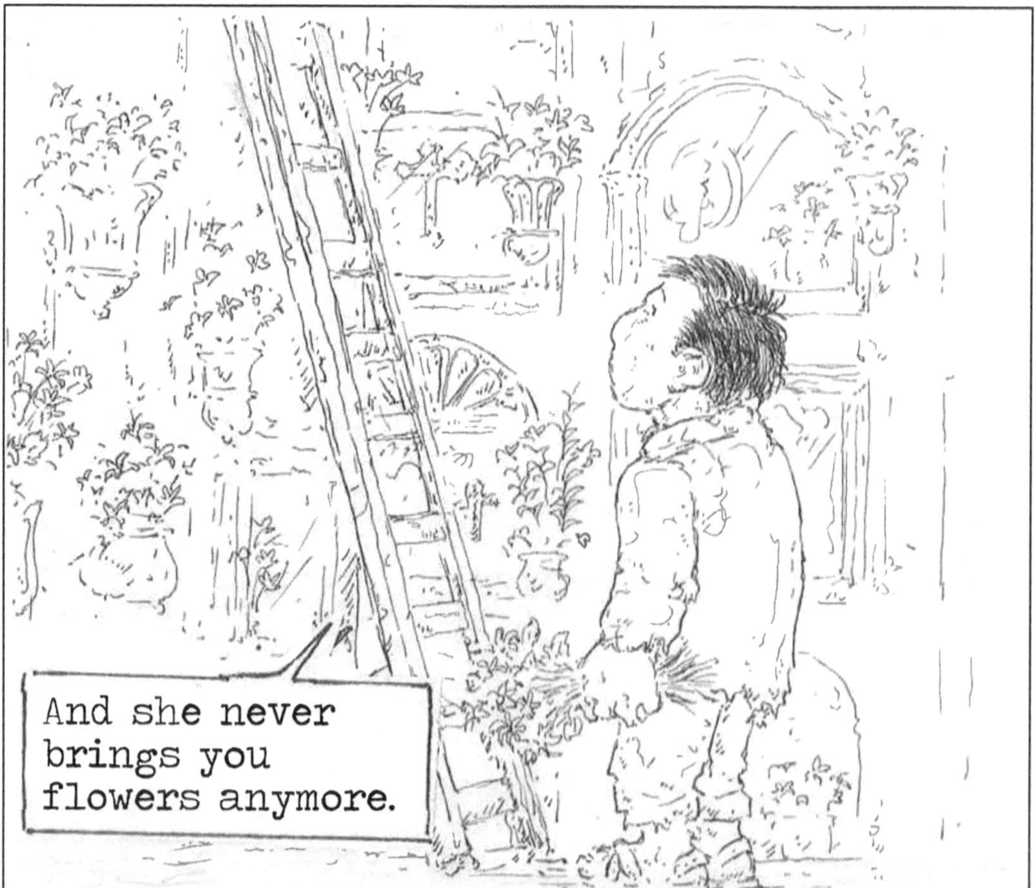

And she never brings you flowers anymore.

I think I am going to run away from home.

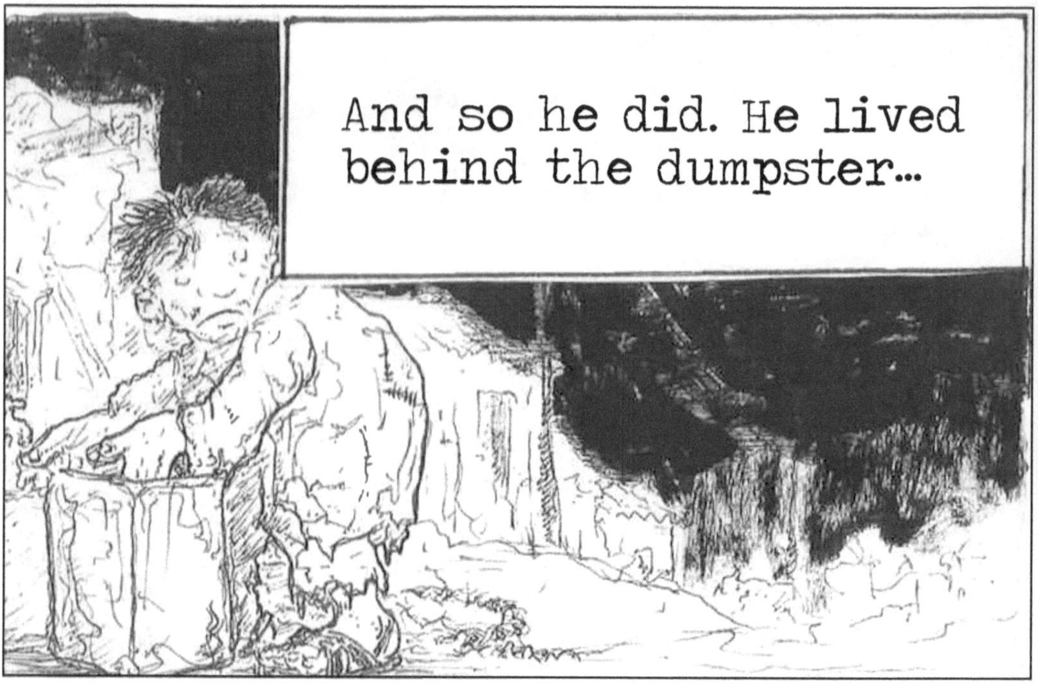

And so he did. He lived behind the dumpster...

Until Don Seferino ran away from his grave.

Be nice!

Little by little,
things began to
improve.

Sometimes they even ate out on Sunday.

Like a real family.

She was actually quite nice when drunk.

Bought Alasito a costume
and gave him a day off.

Alasito had never had any fun in all his life.

So he didn't know where to start.

Where are
your parents?
She thought he was a 
child with big hands.
23

He though he had just met the woman of his dreams.

From then on, he spent all
of his coins on candy,
flowers and chocolate.

Then he would go back to work at the slaughterhouse picking up carcasses and dreamt about the following Sunday...

Once he saw her coming out of the movies.
She looked so beautiful.

And realized it was going to take much more than candy to win her over.

She looked right out of a fairytale. He was penniless, raggedy and smelled like pig's blood.
I have to get myself a comb.
And a bar of soap.

Godmother, could I please have a new shirt for my birthday?

You have no birthday!

That night...

Do I have a birthday?

Of course you do.

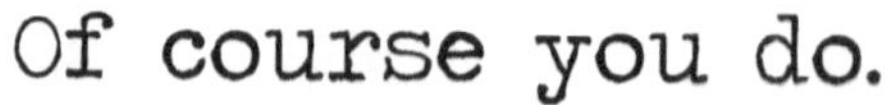

From that day on, he couldn't afford to leave gifts on her doorstep.

He was saving his coins to buy himself a costume.

Days and weeks blurred one into the next, with no time to think.

And the girl began to fear that nobody cared about her anymore.

And he laid the world at her feet.

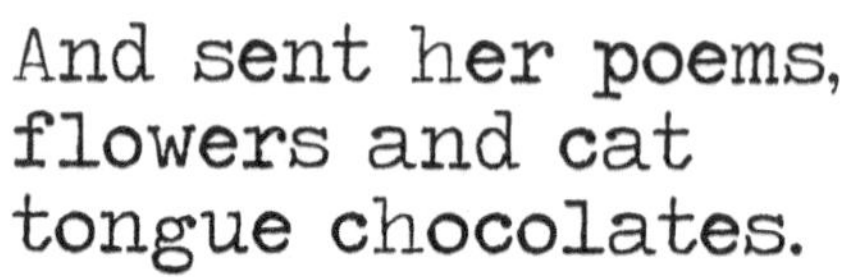

And sent her poems, flowers and cat tongue chocolates.

While Alasito sweated under the twelve o clock sun and ninety pounds of red onions, uphill and with no breakfast.

CARNIVAL

Time passed,
Carnival arrived
and Alasito bought
himself a costume.

Today is goling to be the best day of my life!

63
Thief!
I never thought
you could do
this to me!
41

It was my money

Please godmother.
I just want to
celebrate Carnival.

Thief!

Bitch!

Don't fight!

You are a monster. I will put a curse on you.

I am not a monster.
I am "El Charro de Oro"!

Don't lay a finger on my coffin! I will come back for it one day!

He ran to see her.

And when he arrived...

It was too late.

It sucks to cry when
everybody else is
laughing.

EPILOGUE

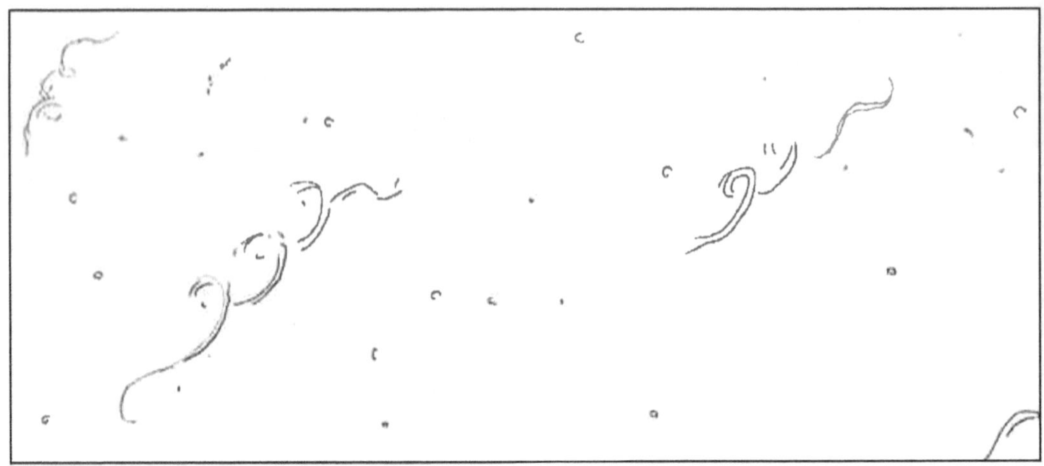

He was feeling sad...

"Don't be afraid to live."

Little by little, mountains and
bad memories were fading away
in the distance...

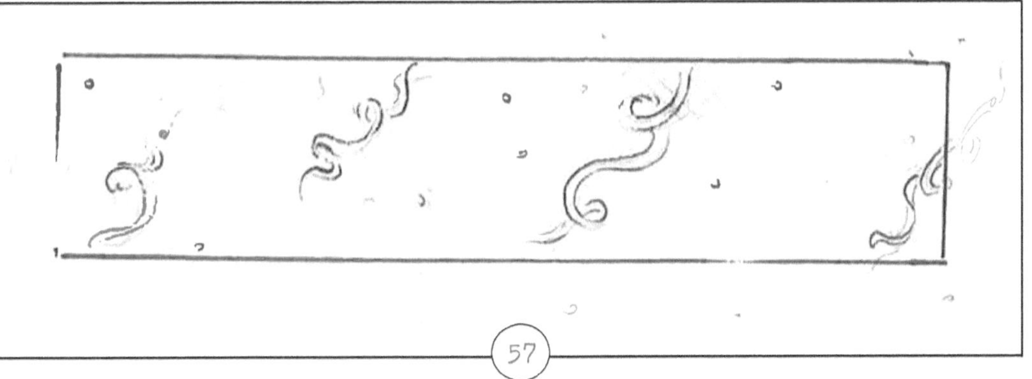

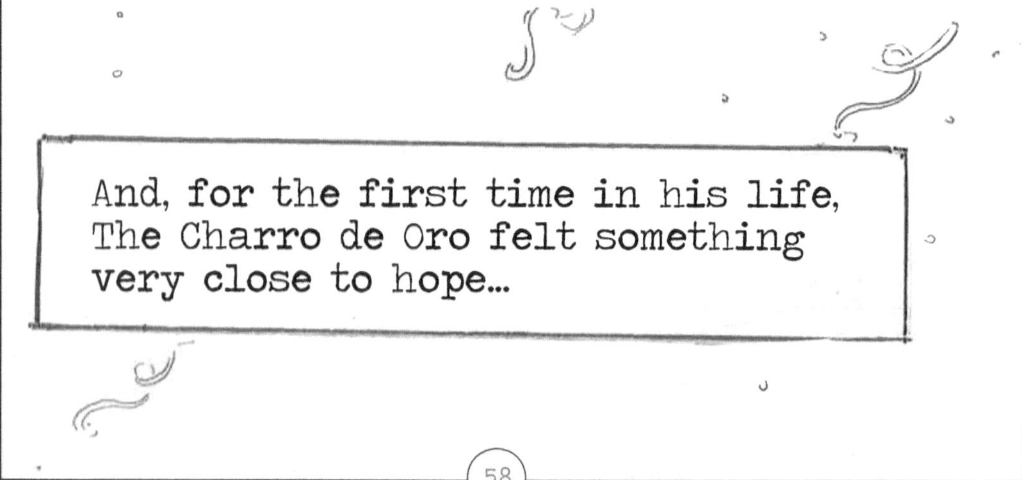

And, for the first time in his life,
The Charro de Oro felt something
very close to hope...

Something very close to happiness.